CONTENTS

1 Shipwrecked and Alone 5

2 Returning to the Wreck 13

3 Building Projects 19

4 More Treasures from the Ship 25

5 Improving Our Home 31

6 Preparing for Winter 40

7 Giving Thanks for Our Blessings . . .46

8 The Stranded Whale 51

9 The Death of a Monster 57

10 Exploring the Island 62

11 Home Again 68

12 Jenny 72

1 Shipwrecked and Alone

The storm had gone on for seven days. Our ship was leaking and far off course. We had no idea where we were. The crew was losing heart as the water rushed in on us.

Every man on board tried to think of some way to survive. My spirits sank as I looked at my wife and four young sons. They were overpowered by terror. "Dear children," I said, "we must trust in God. He can save us from this danger." We knelt down, praying together. Our hearts were soothed by the comfort of prayer. The horror of our situation seemed less overwhelming.

Then I suddenly heard someone cry, "Land, land!" In the next moment, the ship slammed into something hard. Dreadful sounds told us that the ship was breaking up. The roaring waters poured in on all sides.

Then the captain shouted, "Lower away the boats! We are lost!" In minutes, the last of the crew pushed off in the rowboats. They must have forgotten about us! As I called to them for help, my voice was drowned out in the deafening howls of the storm.

Looking around, I saw that our position was by no means hopeless. The part of the ship that held our cabin was jammed between two high rocks. Luckily, it was partly raised above the waves. Through clouds of mist and rain, I could see a rocky, rugged coast. I told my frightened family that as soon as the storm ended, we would make our way to the shore. These few words revived the spirits of the boys and gave them confidence that we would be safe. My wife, however, understood our real situation. The danger was by no means over. That night, as the three youngest boys slept, my wife and I kept watch. Fritz, our eldest son at 15, kept watch with us.

The storm finally ended at dawn. Fritz helped me make a kind of boat. We cut four barrels in half. Then we used long strips of wood to bind them together. While we were doing that, my wife and the other boys did some chores. The animals on the ship needed to be fed. They were frightened and hungry, having been neglected during the storm. The two large dogs in the captain's cabin were thrilled when Jack let them out at last. The following useful animals were also on the ship: a cow, a donkey, two goats, six sheep, a ram, and a fine pig. Then we found that we also had ten hens and two roosters, as well as some ducks, geese, and pigeons.

"These animals are excellent," I said, "but I'm not sure about those big dogs. They'll probably eat more than any of us."

"Oh, Father, they'll be of good use, I'm sure! They'll help us hunt for game when we reach the shore!" Jack exclaimed.

So it was decided that we would take all the animals. Using rollers made from a long mast, we launched our barrel raft. It floated very well. Of course, we had attached it to the ship by a rope. Otherwise, it would have floated away. We took supplies from the ship's stores, including canvas to make a tent. The boys found some carpenter's tools, guns, pistols, powder, bullets, fishing supplies, and an iron pot. We also salvaged some biscuits and powdered soup mix.

Then we all piled into the barrels. My 8-year-old son Franz, the youngest, sat next to my wife. Fritz sat in the next barrel. The center tubs held our supplies, and Ernest and Jack sat toward the back with me. With some difficulty, we learned how to steer our raft with its oars. We followed our geese and ducks to a small bay where it was safe to land. The dogs, who had already swum to shore, greeted us with loud barking and a wild show of delight.

We quickly set up a tent where we could pass the night. The boys collected moss and grass to spread in the tent for our beds. I made a fireplace with some large flat stones from a nearby brook. Soon we had a pot of water boiling. My wife started to make some soup for her hungry family.

The boys went off to explore the area. Soon Jack came back with a big red lobster. We added it to the pot. But how were we to eat the soup? We had no bowls or spoons!

Ernest reported that he'd seen some oysters among the rocks, so he went to get some. I showed the boys how to open oysters. When we placed them on the fire, the shells opened immediately. After eating the oysters, we used the shells as spoons. We ate our soup right from the pot. Later, we would find some coconuts and use the empty shells as bowls.

Night fell quickly. There was little or no twilight—which meant that we were near the equator. I was grateful for the tent, for the night was as cold as the day was hot. Our roosters woke us at dawn, and we had more soup for breakfast. Then Fritz and I left the fire to explore the island. We each took a gun and a game bag, and I carried a small hatchet. Turk, one of the dogs, came with us. We hoped to find some of the ship's sailors, but we could see no trace of them.

We found that our island was a tropical paradise! It had forests of towering trees and fields of sugar cane. There were rolling hills of grass, leafy green plants, and fragrant flowers. We saw brightly colored birds and playful monkeys. As we sat down under some palm trees to eat our simple lunch, I had a good idea. "Watch, Fritz," I said. "I'm going to put those monkeys to work."

With that, I began throwing stones at the tree tops. This made the monkeys angry. They began throwing coconuts down at us. Laughing at the success of my plan, Fritz opened up some of the coconuts with the hatchet. We drank the milk, agreeing that it was refreshing, but not very tasty.

Late that afternoon, we headed back to the tent. We carried a sack of coconuts and a large bundle of sugar cane. We also had a collection of plates, bowls, and spoons that we'd made out of gourds. On the way, we had another incident with the monkeys. Turk attacked a female monkey.

"No, Turk!" Fritz called out—but it was too late! Turk had already killed the monkey. His victim was the mother of a tiny little monkey. It had jumped off her back when Turk attacked. At first, the baby monkey hid in the grass, but then it jumped up on Fritz's shoulder. We decided to take the monkey home as a pet. Because our dog had killed its mother, we felt responsible for its welfare.

As we got near our campsite, our dear ones came running to meet us. The boys shouted in delight, "A monkey! *A monkey!* Oh, how splendid! Where did Fritz find him? What should we feed him? Oh, look at all this sugar cane! Where did you get the coconuts?"

We could neither stop their questions nor get a word in to answer them. Finally, I was able to say a few words. "I'm happy to see you all safe and sound. Sadly, though, we found no trace of our shipmates."

"If it is God's will for us to be alone on this island, let us be content," my wife said. "We should at least be happy that we are all together in safety."

Dinner that night was a feast. We had several fine fish, cooked on a spit over the fire. We also had goose, roasted over a large shell that caught its dripping gravy. In addition, we had cheese, which we'd brought from the ship, along with the last of the soup. "This is not one of our geese," my wife said. "It's a wild bird Ernest killed today."

We sat down for our delicious meal, using

our gourds as plates for the first time. We had coconuts for dessert. Fritz laughed as the baby monkey eagerly sucked the corner of a handkerchief he had dipped in coconut milk.

The sun set quickly, and we decided to go to sleep. We weren't asleep for very long, though, when a loud barking woke us. Jackals were coming near, hoping to kill and eat some of our poultry. Turk and Juno, our brave dogs, were surrounded by a dozen or more of the wild creatures. We saw that the dogs had already killed four of the jackals, but the others kept fighting. Fritz and I shot our guns in the air, and the rest ran off.

Turk and Juno chased after them and killed one more. Fritz dragged one of the jackals toward the tent. He wanted to show it to his brothers in the morning. Once more we returned to our beds.

2 Returning to the Wreck

My wife and I woke up early. We started to talk about the business of the day.

"I think Fritz and I should return to the wreck while the sea is still calm," I said. "We must save the poor animals that are still there. We also need to get more supplies from the ship. If we don't get to them now, we may lose them entirely."

"Yes—by all means," my wife agreed. "While you're gone, the other boys and I will look for a better place to make our home. Come, let us wake the boys and get to work."

Fritz was the first to get up. He ran outside to get his dead jackal. It was cold and stiff from the night air. He propped it on its legs by the tent. The dogs growled at it, but Fritz called them off.

"It's a yellow dog!" Franz cried.

"A wolf!" Jack exclaimed.

"No, it's a striped fox," Ernest said.

"You're all partly correct," I said. "This is a jackal. It's from the same family as the dog, the wolf, and the fox."

When the monkey saw the jackal, it hid itself in a heap of moss inside the tent. Jack soothed and comforted the little animal. Then we sat down to a good breakfast of biscuits, butter, and cheese. As we ate, I noticed that the dogs seemed very quiet. I soon discovered the cause. The night before, they'd been hurt in the fight with the jackals. They had several deep and painful wounds, especially on their necks. The dogs began to lick each other on the places they couldn't reach with their own tongues.

Suddenly Ernest had an idea. He said the dogs needed spiked collars, and that he could make them. With spiked collars, he explained, they could avoid getting the same kinds of wounds again. I told Ernest this sounded like a good idea and that he should try it. I suggested that he could make the collars from leather and use nails for the spikes. Maybe we could find the supplies on the wreck.

Then I told Fritz that he and I would be visiting the wreck today. Next, I worked out a set of signals with my wife so we could communicate while Fritz and I were gone. I tied a wide strip of cloth on a pole and raised it high in the air. As long as all was well, I explained to my wife, the flag should stay up. If she needed us to return, she would lower the flag and fire three shots.

Fritz and I soon left in our barrel boat, taking the monkey with us. Fritz wanted to get milk for it as soon as possible. The current quickly carried us to the wreck. By the time we got on board, we could hear the animals greeting us. They weren't hungry, for they still had plenty of food. They were just happy to see us. When Fritz put the monkey by one of the goats, the little animal immediately helped himself to some goat milk.

Fritz and I then put a mast and a sail on our barrel boat. "The current that brought us here will not take us back. But that fresh breeze will!" I explained. By the time we got the sail ready, it was getting late. We signaled our plan to stay on board for the night.

The rest of the day was spent stowing supplies on the boat. We took gunpowder, guns, and a whole armful of swords, daggers, and knives. We also took kitchen supplies, including more pots, knives, and forks. We packed canned meats, powdered soups, hams, sausages, wheat, and all the other seeds and vegetables we could find. We found some rope, nails, tools, and farming supplies. Finally, nothing more could be squeezed into our little boat.

Soon it was time to sleep. Fritz fell asleep easily, but I had trouble. For hours I tossed and turned. I was worried about my wife and children, alone and unprotected, except by the dogs.

At last morning came. I looked toward shore and was happy to see my little flag still waving. To get the animals to shore, we had to figure out a way to keep them afloat. So we made life jackets for them. Each life jacket was made of two empty barrels, one on either side of the animal. These were tied together by leather thongs. We tied a large cork

underneath for buoyancy. One by one, the animals were fitted into their jackets and pushed into the sea. As each animal bobbed back to the surface, it slowly began swimming toward the shore.

On the way, we saw a shark trying to attack one of the sheep! Fritz quickly stopped the attack by firing two shots to the beast's head. Leaving a bloody trail, the dying animal slowly turned in the water and swam away.

At last we all reached land safely. My wife and the boys came running out to greet us.

That night we had a truly wonderful feast. This time my wife even used a tablecloth and silverware! During dinner, she told me about her day. She and the boys had done some exploring, as they searched for a safer place. She wanted to build a tree house among a grove of trees. High up in the air, we'd be safe from jackals and other dangerous animals. And there we'd also have shade, which would keep us cooler in the daytime.

I agreed that this was a very good idea. Our next problem was moving. How would we transport all our supplies and animals to the new location? We'd have to cross a river to get to the grove of trees. The solution was simple—but it wouldn't be easy. First, we'd need to build a bridge!

Building Projects

It didn't take us as long as we'd thought to build the bridge. First, the animals helped us haul the wooden planks that had washed up from our wrecked ship. Then we used a pulley system to help the mule and the cow get the planks into place. Our new bridge seemed quite solid. The children could hardly contain their excitement. They danced to and fro on our wonderful bridge, singing and shouting.

The next morning, we loaded all of our supplies on the cow and the mule. Then, with each of us carrying a gun and a sack of goods, we were ready to go. The little monkey, which we had named Knips, rode on Turk's back. He made funny faces as he bounced along. All the other animals trailed behind us.

Once across the bridge, we passed through fields of high grass. Then the dogs ran off and we soon heard them howling loudly—as if in pain. Jack ran toward them to see what was wrong. "Father! Father! Come quickly!" he called. "It's a porcupine!"

Sure enough, the dogs had tried to attack a porcupine. Both dogs were badly hurt by the quills. Jack took out his pistol and shot the porcupine dead. Then he carefully wrapped his handkerchief around its neck and dragged it to where his mother was waiting. He was very proud of it. "Look, mother, I shot it! Do you think it's good to eat?" he said.

Smiling at the child's eagerness, I wrapped the porcupine in several folds of cloth. Then I piled it on top of the donkey's load. After that small excitement, we continued our march until we reached the site of our future home.

The grove of trees was truly wonderful. The trees seemed to be mangroves or wild figs. They had huge, arching roots that supported the main trunk above the soil. The calm beauty of the spot was just as splendid as my wife had told me. I promised her that our next house would be the safest and most charming place in the whole world!

We unloaded the mule and the cow. We secured them, as well as the sheep and goats, by loosely tying their front feet together. We set the doves and poultry free before we finally sat down to rest.

After a while, Ernest gathered some large, flat stones to build a fireplace. Franz went off in another direction to gather sticks for the fire. He soon came back, eating a fig.

"Where did you find that?" I asked.

"There are thousands of them lying in the grass over there!" Franz reported. "They're delicious. Look—the pigeons and the hens are already gobbling them up."

"Well, if birds and monkeys eat a fruit or vegetable, it's usually safe for humans, too. But in the future, please don't eat anything unless you show it to me first."

We ate porcupine for our dinner that night. Some we boiled and some we roasted. By boring holes at the ends of the porcupine's quills, I made some needles for my wife's sewing. Then I thought about how to make a harness for our beasts of burden.

We had to build a ladder to reach the

tallest branches of our tree. Ernest suggested that we use bamboo for the rungs of the ladder. That worked just fine. We attached the cut bamboo to rope until the ladder was long enough. How would I get it up to the highest branches? I had a good idea! Using a bow and arrow, I shot the end of a ball of string over the branch. Then I tied one end of the string to the ladder. By pulling the other end of the string, I raised the ladder up to the branch. After scrambling up the tree trunk and out onto the branch, the boys tied the ladder tight. Then I climbed up the ladder to attach a pulley to the tree trunk. Now the pulley and our beasts of burden could help us haul lumber up the tree!

We used wood from the shipwreck to build our house. The big tree we had chosen was perfect! Its branches grew very close together in a horizontal direction. We built a floor on the first level. On each side, we made a wall about four feet high out of planks. Six feet or so above the floor, we hung our hammocks in boughs. Then we threw the sail cloth over the higher branches to make a roof. Finally, we pulled the cloth down and nailed it to the wooden wall on two sides. The tree trunk itself formed the back wall of our house. The front was left open to the fresh air.

I built a big table at the foot of the tree. This was where we would eat our meals.

The next morning at breakfast I said, "Let's name our home and the different parts of the island." Everyone was excited. They thought that was a wonderful idea.

"How about a name for the bay where we first landed?" I asked.

"Let's call it Oyster Bay," Fritz suggested. "Remember all the oysters I found there?"

"No, it should be Lobster Bay," Jack shouted. "That's where I got the lobster."

My wife suggested the name Providence Bay. "To thank God for getting all of us here safely," she said. So Providence Bay it was.

We called our first home Tent House, and we named our tree house Falcon's Nest. The swamp, where many flamingoes lived, was called Flamingo Marsh. The stream that divided the island was named Jackal River, and we named our bridge Family Bridge. We also decided to name our island. We called it New Switzerland.

Once we had decided on these names, we began to feel much more at home.

The following day, Ernest and I went fishing in Providence Bay. There, he caught a huge fish. We were on our way home when our dog Juno chased after a strange animal. The beast was making extraordinary jumps toward us! Ernest lifted his gun and shot the animal dead.

"Look at it!" Ernest cried. "He's the size of a sheep, but he has the tail of a tiger. His nose and hair look something like a mouse's, but his ears are like a rabbit's! His front legs are like those of a squirrel, but his back legs are like the tallest stilts! Whatever can it be?"

"I think it's a kangaroo, son," I said. "See the pouch on the front of its body? Its young hide there for safety."

We brought the fish and the kangaroo home. That night, we cooked the fish and part of the kangaroo, saving the rest for salting. Then, with thankful hearts, we went to bed and enjoyed a well-earned sleep.

4 More Treasures from the Ship

Next morning, I took care of the beautiful kangaroo hide. I wanted to preserve the whole thing. After that, Fritz and I decided to go out to the ship to get some more supplies. I knew that with the first storm, the ship would break up. We had to get as much as we could before then. I left my wife and the other three boys at home, with the dogs for protection. Fritz and I planned to stay overnight on the ship.

We reached the ship without too much difficulty. The first thing we did was build a raft to carry things. As a base, we used 12 empty water barrels. We tied them together with spars and strong rope. Then we put down a floor of sturdy planks. In this way we fashioned ourselves a first-rate raft, just right for our needs.

We made our supper from the ship's

provisions. Then we slept on mattresses. This seemed like quite a luxury after sleeping in our narrow hammocks!

The next morning we loaded the raft and our barrel boat. This time we took the contents of our own cabin and the furniture from the captain's room. We even took the doors, window frames, bolts, bars, and locks. We emptied the officers' chests and those of the carpenter and gunsmith. Fritz was delighted to find a chest full of gold and silver watches, rings, and money. But far more useful to us was a full set of knives and forks!

We were thrilled to find a number of young fruit trees, still carefully packed away. Each tree was clearly labeled: apple, pear, chestnut, orange, almond, peach, apricot, plum, and cherry. How wonderful it would be to grow our own fruit on the island!

The cargo had been destined for a distant colony. It included iron goods, plumber's tools, lead, paint, grindstones, cart wheels, spades, and plows. We also found sacks of corn, peas, oats, and wheat. There was a hand mill and parts of a sawmill that we could assemble later. We loaded all these items onto our raft. We filled up our last remaining space with fishing lines, reels, and harpoons.

At last we set out for the trip back to land. With so many goods piled on the raft, there was some danger of an accident. But the sea was calm and the wind was in our favor. We made good progress.

Suddenly, Fritz saw a huge turtle floating on the water. He quickly threw a harpoon, and the point landed in the turtle's flesh. The wounded animal headed toward land, pulling our boat and raft along with it. Afraid of losing our goods, I grabbed my hatchet. I wanted to cut the line and cast off the turtle and the harpoon. But Fritz begged me to wait. "There is no danger yet, Father! If necessary, I promise to cut the line myself. Let's catch this turtle if we can!"

I agreed to wait and see what happened. After pulling us all the way to shore, the turtle tried to get away. I leaped into the water and waded up to it. Then I killed the turtle with my hatchet.

My wife and the boys were running toward

the beach to welcome us back. The sight of
the turtle, along with the well-packed raft and
boat, surprised them all. We took some of the
supplies, along with the turtle, back to
Falcon's Nest.

My wife cooked some of the turtle meat
for dinner. Then Fritz told us about his idea
for using the turtle shell. We could keep it
near the brook and use it as a basin! Just that
day, Jack had found some clay. He suggested
that we use it to build a firm foundation for
the turtle shell.

Then Ernest told us about something he'd found that day. He had noticed the pig eating something she'd found under a small bush. It turned out to be manioc root. I told the children that the manioc root would be very useful. If we had no other food than that, we would never starve! Flour could be made from these roots, and then used to make some special cakes called cassava bread. These flat cakes were quite delicious when cooked in a pan. The only difficulty was getting all the juice out of the root—for this liquid was poisonous! Before we ate them, the manioc roots would have to be carefully grated, squeezed, and pressed until dry.

We spent the next morning moving all the supplies from the beach to our tree house. In the afternoon, Fritz, Jack, and I went back to the ship to salvage more goods. Jack was thrilled to hunt about in the hold, looking for useful things. He found a wheelbarrow, which would surely be very handy. But his best find was a small sailing ship! Its separate parts had been carefully packed in a huge box. There were even two small brass guns to mount on the ship. This was a truly great discovery!

It took us several days, but we finally put together the small sailing ship. Then we launched it, using a system of rollers, levers, and pulleys. My wife was quite surprised when she saw us returning to land on such a fine ship! After we anchored and moored the vessel, we stood back to admire her. Her elegant appearance had really changed the looks of our harbor! Now, in addition to our barrel boat and our flat, uninteresting raft, we had a beautiful sailboat!

Then my wife showed me what she had been doing while we were away. It was a neat garden, laid out in beds and walks! She had planted lettuce, cabbages, beans, peas, and potatoes. Beyond the garden was a clearing large enough for sugar cane and the young fruit trees, too. I was very pleased with my wife's work. Later, I would set up a watering system I'd already been designing in my mind. I planned to use hollow bamboo as pipelines to carry water from the falls.

5 Improving Our Home

The next morning, my wife asked me to plant the little fruit trees. "I fear they've been too long neglected," she said. "Yesterday I watered them and spread earth over the roots, but I couldn't plant them."

"You've done more than enough already, my dear wife," I said.

The three older boys and I spent the rest of the day planting the trees. We used stalks of bamboo to support the slim, young trunks until they could grow stronger.

"This would be a good place to house our hens and pigeons," I said, looking around. "I could make coops for them out of gourds and put them in the trees. Up there, they'd be safe from the jackals and other dangers."

But that project would have to wait. We spent the next week or so making many trips

31

back to the wreck. Finally, we'd removed every single thing that was useful.

Since we had taken all we could from it, I decided to sink the wreck. The next day, Fritz, Jack, Ernest, and I sailed out and put a cask of gunpowder on the deck. We lit it just before sailing away. By the time we reached shore, the ship blew up. That was an emotional moment for all of us. Our isolation seemed final now. We all began to wonder if we would ever see our beloved Switzerland again.

By the next morning, however, our sorrow turned to delight. Now our beach was littered with planks and boards from the ruined ship. This lumber, of course, would be very useful.

That very day we decided to explore the interior of the island. I wanted to know of any dangers we hadn't yet discovered. I also wanted to look for anything else we could use. We all set off in the morning. Our cow and Grizzle, our donkey, pulled a sled piled high with our equipment. We brought a tent, food, and ammunition—enough for a stay of several days. The two dogs, Turk and Juno, came running after us.

Our path led us through one forest after another. The trees were the most unusual we had ever seen! I saw a guava tree, whose fruit looked like our apple. I also saw a candleberry tree. I had once read that boiling its heavy berries produced a form of candle wax. Fritz was the first to notice some India rubber trees. I punched a hole in one of these trees and put down a gourd to catch its milky sap. Later, I could use this sap to make waterproof boots and shoes.

We found oak trees with sweet-tasting acorns. Then Ernest tasted the beans from some cocoa trees. They were delicious! He quickly stuffed his pockets full of the dark brown beans. "These can be used to make a tasty chocolate drink!" he said.

That evening, we set up camp and made our supper. We freed Grizzle to graze. But as we were eating, Grizzle suddenly pricked up his ears, brayed loudly, and ran off! We followed a short way, and then I sent the dogs to chase him. But they came back later without our donkey! Since darkness was falling, we had to give up for the night.

I was worried about Grizzle, but I was also worried for the rest of us us. Had Grizzle sensed the approach of some fierce wild animal? I said nothing of my concerns to my family. Instead, I made a large fire to frighten away any dangers. Then we all went to sleep.

In the morning, I rose early and looked out, hoping to see Grizzle. But there was no sign of him. After breakfast, Jack and I, along with the two dogs, set off to find Grizzle. I left Fritz and Ernest to protect their mother.

For an hour or so we followed the prints of Grizzle's hooves. Then we saw that he seemed to have joined a herd of larger animals, and we lost his trail. I almost gave up, but Jack urged me to keep on looking. At last we came upon a herd of buffaloes. They stared at us, without moving. We began to back away, but the dogs dashed ahead and attacked a buffalo calf! This made the whole herd rush forward to attack us. I shot and killed the leader. The sound of the gunshot made the rest of the buffaloes run away.

The dogs were still fighting with the calf, but they couldn't bring him to the ground. I

decided to save the young bull's life. My thought was that we could tame him to use as a beast of burden. We called off the dogs. Then Jack used a lasso to catch the animal by his hind legs.

"Now that we have him," Jack said, "what will we do with him?"

"I'll show you," I said. "Help me keep his front legs together. Then watch what I do." Once tied, the bull could not move. I told Jack to hold the bull's head. Then I used a knife to cut through the inside of the animal's nose. I passed a rope through the hole. I did not like to hurt the poor beast, but it was necessary. Finally, we freed the animal and pulled on the rope. He followed us without resisting.

After cutting a couple of big steaks from the dead buffalo, I packed them in salt. The rest I left for the dogs.

On the way back to our campsite, Juno and Turk ran ahead. Suddenly, we heard yelps. They were being attacked by a jackal! From the fierce way the jackal fought, I realized that her young might be nearby. After the dogs won the fight, Jack asked if he could take one of the young jackals home. He named his new pet Fangs.

The other children were delighted by our new animals. To them, these animals were a good exchange for the loss of our poor donkey.

For dinner that night, we ate buffalo steaks. Ernest told us about a young eagle he had seen that day. I suggested that he capture it and train it to hunt as a falcon. Ernest liked that idea. The next day he managed to throw a cloth over the bird's head! Unable to see, the young eagle was quite easy to catch.

The next day we returned to Falcon's Nest. I thought it unfair to make the cow pull everything, so I hitched up the young buffalo to take Grizzle's place. Ernest carried his young eagle, which he had blindfolded for the trip. On the way, we stopped to get some berries from the candleberry tree. We would make candles when we got back. We also took enough India rubber sap to make some waterproof shoes and boots.

After we got home, my wife asked me to build a staircase to the tree house. It was too hard for her to climb up and down the rope ladder all the time. Knowing that bees lived inside the tree, I thought it might be somewhat hollow already.

First, we blew smoke into the tree to calm the bees down. Then we were able to remove the bees, hives and all. After that, we stopped up the holes in the trunk so the bees could not return. In that way, we forced them to move into the hollow gourds we had provided as a new home. Finally, we harvested their honey for future use.

Now we were able to turn the inside of the tree into a staircase. We cut an opening to fit the door we had brought from the captain's cabin. Then we hung the door, hinges and all. We cleared the rotten wood from the center of the tree and put the trunk of a young tree inside. Now we could use this trunk as the center of our spiral staircase! We cut notches in the trunk of the young tree and then cut corresponding notches in the old tree. Then we fitted wooden steps into these notches, nailing them in tight. As we built the staircase, we also cut windows in the outer trunk to let in light and air. It took us a full month—but we finally had an inside staircase! It led from the ground floor all the way to the top of our tree house.

Meanwhile, our animals were busy having babies. The pig had a litter of seven piglets. The hens had 40 chicks, the goats had two kids, and the sheep had five lambs. With these births and our garden, it was clear that we would never be without food.

Juno had a litter of puppies as well. She also accepted the baby jackal as part of her litter, so we didn't have to worry about him.

I then turned to the job of making shoes. First, I filled a pair of socks with sand. Then I coated them over with clay to form a mold. After the clay hardened in the sun, I brushed layer after layer of India rubber over it. I made sure that each layer dried before applying the next one. Then I dried them in the sun, broke out the clay, and attached a strip of buffalo hide to the soles. After brushing the buffalo hide with India rubber, I had a good pair of waterproof boots.

I was delighted. Orders poured in from all sides. Soon everyone in the family had a pair.

Our next big project was to channel fresh water closer to our tree house. We began by making a dam in the river upstream. Then we led the water down by bamboo pipes. It flowed into the turtle's shell that we had saved. The extra water flowed off through the hole made by Fritz's harpoon. This promised to be a great time-saver. Now we no longer had to carry water from the stream every day.

6 Preparing for Winter

One evening we were surprised by Grizzle's return! He was with a female animal that looked very much like him. She was an onager, a type of wild donkey. When Grizzle came close to get some food from my hand, his partner came closer. Fritz put a rope around her neck. He had already tied one end of the rope to a tree. When the animal saw that she was tied, she got very angry. She cast fiery glances all around and lashed out with her hooves. She struggled to get free. But the rope was strong, and her efforts were in vain. Finally, she calmed down. To comfort the frightened animal, we tied Grizzle nearby and left them for the night.

In the morning she was as wild as ever. How could I tame her proud spirit? Suddenly, I remembered an old trick of the American

Indians. I jumped on the onager's back and bit down on her ear. The animal immediately stood still! From that moment, we were her masters. The children soon learned to ride her. After that, she carried them wherever they wanted to go.

I soon realized that it was time to prepare for the rainy season. Our tree house, open on one side, would not provide enough shelter. We also needed some kind of shelter for our animals during the winter.

We covered the vaulted roots of our tree, making the frame from bamboo canes. We used clay and moss to fill in the open spaces. Then we covered the whole thing with a mixture of tar and lime water. We divided the area into several parts. Now, under one roof, we had dry places for ourselves and all the animals. All we had yet to do was store the food. We worked day after day, bringing in ripe food of all kinds. We collected potatoes, coconuts, sweet acorns, and sugar canes. Then thunder and dark skies warned us that we had no time to lose.

It began to rain. We could no longer stay

in our tree house. It was time to retreat to the trunk. After we carried our furniture down, our dwelling was very crowded. But by packing more efficiently, we made enough room for working and sleeping.

Winter was long and boring. In the mornings we took care of the animals. The boys took care of their pets. We'd made lots of wax candles earlier, so we could light up our room at night. I wrote a journal of all the adventures we'd had since being shipwrecked. My wife was kept busy sewing clothes for us all. Ernest made sketches of the birds, beasts, and flowers on the island. Fritz and Jack taught little Franz to read.

Week after week rolled by. Day after day, hard rain fell around us. A feeling of constant gloom hung over the scene.

At last spring arrived. No prisoners could have felt more joy than we did at being set free! The seeds we had sown were now growing up through the moist earth! All of nature was refreshed.

We cleaned up our tree house. In a few days we moved back in. Then we went to see how Tent House had survived the winter. Sadly, it was ruined. The canvas had blown down and been ripped into rags. The supplies we had left there were soaked.

The sailboat and the raft were safe, but the barrel boat had been dashed into pieces.

Fritz suggested that we hollow out a big cave in the rock. We could put some of our supplies there. I thought that was a good idea. It took us 10 days to make a small dent in the rock. But suddenly, one of Fritz's tools went right through the rock and crashed down inside! We realized then that only a thin wall lay between us and a great cavern.

Before long we had chipped out a hole big enough for us to enter. As I stood near the opening, I noticed that the air inside was very stale. I told my sons to stay away. "Unless air moves around, it becomes poisonous. Fire is the safest way to restore this place to its clean state," I told them. We lit some hay and threw it in the cavern. When the fire went out, the air was safe to breathe.

The inside of the cave had walls of glittering crystal. Our candles reflected a golden light. The floor of this beautiful rock palace was hard, dry sand. I saw at once that we could live inside the cave without any fear of danger from dampness.

I tasted a piece of the crystal. It was a cavern of rock salt! There was no doubt about it. We had found an unlimited supply of the best and purest salt.

Our minds were full of wonder as we went back to Falcon's Nest. Along the way, we couldn't stop talking about the new house. We soon decided to use Falcon's Nest as a summer home and the salt cave as our winter home.

The next day, we cut a row of large holes in the rock to let in light and air. Into these holes we put the windows we had taken from the officers' cabins. Then we brought the door from Falcon's Nest and fitted it into the cave opening. The opening in the tree trunk I hid with bark. This would discourage wild beasts from coming in while we were away.

We divided the cave into four parts. The first was for our sleeping and eating areas. The second was for our kitchen and workshop. The third was for our stables. We decided to use the fourth part as our storehouse. Then we built a fireplace and chimney so the smoke from our fires could escape.

Next, we spent many weeks near the cave making a farm for our animals. We could keep our stable animals with us in the cave. But the other animals also needed shelter. After a great deal of work, we had several safe shelters close to the cave. This would be the most comfortable island home we had lived in yet! We named it Rock House.

We soon found that the surrounding area offered an endless supply of fish and game. Huge turtles visited the shore to lay their eggs. Great schools of fish swam in the bay.

One afternoon we came upon a grove of bushes that appeared to be covered with snowflakes. Looking closer, I found that the snowflakes were really puffs of cotton! We gathered all the plants we could and brought them back to the cave. My wife planted some cuttings in her garden! She used the cotton we had already harvested to make new clothes for us all.

Giving Thanks for Our Blessings

7

"You know," I said one afternoon to my wife, "tomorrow is an important day for us. Do you realize that it will mark our second anniversary on the island?"

"Oh! Can that really be true?" my wife exclaimed. "I can hardly believe it."

"It is true, my dear," I said. "Think of how very good God has been to us! That's why I'm going to declare tomorrow a holiday—a special day of celebration."

The next day we had a feast to celebrate our great good fortune. We also had contests among the boys. For two years, they'd been practicing wrestling, running, swimming, shooting, and horseback riding. Now we would see which of them was the champion in each sport.

Fritz turned out to be the champion

swimmer and most expert shot. He received a fine English rifle and hunting knife as his rewards. Ernest, as the best runner, got a gold watch. Jack got silver spurs and a riding whip for his outstanding donkey-riding talent. And Franz, for his skill in riding the buffalo, received a pair of stirrups and a driving whip.

When the ceremony was over, I gave my good wife a lovely workbox. It was filled with a collection of fine needles and other sewing supplies. She was surprised and delighted.

The next day we were all back at work. Again, the rainy season was coming.

The boys caught many kinds of fish, which we preserved by salting. Now that we had the salt cave, this was no problem. Our supply of salt would last a long time. We also went out and gathered bag after bag of sweet acorns to add to our winter store.

For some time, nothing special happened. Then one day, Jack got into some trouble. He had left early that morning on one of his private expeditions. This had become his habit. He always enjoyed surprising us with some new discovery on his return.

This time, however, Jack had no smile on his face when he returned. He was covered with mud and green slime! He had lost a shoe, and he looked miserable.

I was concerned. "My dear boy, what happened to you?" I asked.

"I was walking in the swamp, Father," he explained. "I went to gather reeds so I could make some baskets and coops for the hens. A little way off in the marsh, I saw some good reeds. They were much better than those near the edge, so I went after them.

"I tried to jump from one spot to another. But my foot slipped, and I sank in over my ankles. I tried to get closer to the reeds, which were not far from me. But I kept sinking deeper and deeper until I was up to my knees in thick, soft mud. I was stuck!

"I screamed and called out, but nobody came. I was very scared. At last, who should appear but Fangs, my faithful jackal! He came up close to me, but all he could do was make more noise. No one heard us, though. No matter how I struggled, I kept sinking deeper and deeper! I couldn't get out. Finally, I cut down all the reeds I could reach and tied them together in a bundle. Then I leaned on this bundle while I kicked about to free my feet and legs. At long last, I finally got astride the reeds.

"I sat there resting for a while, supported above the mud and slime. Fangs kept running back and forth between me and the bank. He seemed surprised that I didn't follow him! Suddenly, I thought of catching hold of his tail. When he next came to me, I did just that. As he dragged and pulled, I crawled and waded, using my reeds like a raft. Finally, we got back to dry land."

"A lucky escape for you, my boy!" I cried. "I thank God for it! Fangs is a hero, and it's a good thing he was with you! Now go and get clean. That slimy mud will be hard to wash off. And thank you for bringing me these splendid reeds. They're exactly what I needed for a new plan I have in mind."

The fact was, I wanted to make a loom for my wife. The reeds Jack had brought worked perfectly! A week or so later, I presented my wife with the loom. She was very pleased.

Now she could weave cloth, which she could use to make clothing for all of us.

The boys and I spent the next few weeks gathering food for the winter. We carried many loads of roots, fruits, grains, potatoes, rice, acorns, and pine cones to the cavern. At last we were ready for another winter.

8 The Stranded Whale

Snug in our new Rock House, we were not as bored as we had been the previous winter. We had many projects to keep us busy and plenty of room to work. We hung up a ship's lantern to give us light. After Ernest and Franz put up shelves for our library, we unpacked the books we had taken from the wreck. There were books of voyages, travels, and natural history. And there were history and science books, as well as fiction in several languages. There were also maps, charts, and a pair of globes.

Fritz and I set up a fine workshop. The carpenter's bench was put into place. All of our tools and instruments were neatly hung on the walls.

We still needed so many things! We built shelves, tables, benches, and movable steps. We also made cupboards, pegs, door handles, and bolts. At home in Switzerland, we had taken all these things for granted! Now we had to use imagination and hard work to get the same comforts.

In reality, however, the more there was to do, the better it was for us. Our adventures on the island had taught me that working toward goals is the main element of happiness!

We made a wide porch along the front of the cave and sheltered it with bamboo.

Sometimes we would amuse ourselves by opening chests and packages that had not yet been touched. Many treasures were brought to light. We found mirrors, wardrobes, and tables with marble tops. We also found some writing tables and good chairs, several clocks, and a music box. Soon our winter home was fitted up like a palace!

It seemed that the rainy season went by quickly. Time didn't hang heavy on anyone's hands. Soon it was spring again.

We were glad to be able to leave the cave. Once again we were free to roam in the open air. We crossed Jackal River one day and were walking along the coast. Then Fritz saw

something on the small island near Flamingo Marsh. From our point of view, it looked like an overturned boat!

We decided to get closer to see what we could find. It was not a boat! The enormous object turned out to be a huge whale that had become stranded and then died.

"What a huge brute!" Fritz cried. "He's ever so much larger than he seemed from a distance! How can we use this huge carcass?"

"You'd be surprised at the many ways an animal such as this can be useful," I said. "For one thing, it can supply us with oil to use in our lantern."

We immediately returned to Rock House to get the tools we would need. The next day we went back to the island near Flamingo Marsh. The whole family came along, as we had much work to do. We had so many things to carry! We brought all the barrels and casks that we could squeeze into the boat. We also took knives and hatchets. Since the wind was with us, we soon landed close to the whale.

Its enormous size astonished my wife and our youngest boy. The creature was 60 to 65 feet long and 30 to 40 feet around. Its weight could not have been less than 50,000 pounds!

The whale was black in color. Its huge head was about one-third the length of the entire body. The eyes were quite small—not much larger than those of an ox. Its ears were almost impossible to see.

The animal's huge jaw was nearly 16 feet long. The most interesting part of the great beast was the substance known as whalebone. This whalebone appeared all along both jaws. It was solid at the base, but toward the top it was split into a kind of fringe.

The tongue was quite large, soft, and full of oil. Strangely, the opening of the throat was very small—only about two inches wide!

"Look at that narrow throat! Whatever can this great creature eat?" Fritz exclaimed. "He could never swallow a proper mouthful of food!"

"Let me explain it to you," I said. "This huge animal eats just the smallest of sea creatures. Only shrimps, tiny fish, lobsters, and other small creatures form his diet. The whale drives with open mouth through areas where these creatures live. He takes them into his mouth by the millions! When his mouth is full of prey, he closes his jaws. Next, he forces the water out through the whalebone—but the captured animals cannot get through the fringe! Then he can swallow them at his leisure. And now, boys, let me see you climb this slippery mountain of flesh. It's time to cut it up."

Fritz and Jack got started right away. First, they helped me cut away the lips, so we could get to the whalebone. Then Ernest worked at the creature's side, cutting out big slabs of blubber. My wife and Franz helped as well as they could to put everything in casks.

It took us several days of hard work to get everything useful from the whale. We even took some of the skin to turn into leather for harnesses and such. When we had taken all we could, we left the whale's remains to the birds of prey. With a full cargo, we set sail for land.

We were glad to get home. We needed to rest, because we had a lot of work to do the next day. A refreshing bath, clean clothes, and a good supper cheered us all. That night we slept in peace.

The next morning, we began to boil the blubber in big tubs. Then we skimmed and strained the water through a coarse cloth. In this manner, we obtained an ample supply of excellent oil. After pouring it into bottles, we stored the oil in our back storeroom. Now we had enough oil to keep our lanterns burning for many years.

9 The Death of a Monster

I was seated with Fritz and my wife on the porch in front of Rock House. We were chatting pleasantly when Fritz suddenly got up. He looked off in the distance, and exclaimed, "What's that over there, Father? First it seems to coil on the ground like a cable. Then it rises up as if it were a little mast. Then it sinks, and the coils move along again. It's coming this way!"

I took my spyglass and looked through it. Just as I feared, it was an enormous snake! "It's coming this way," I cried. "Thank God, we're here at Rock House. Get everyone inside, Fritz, including the animals. Then we'll look for a chance to kill this enemy."

I watched as the snake came closer. From time to time, it raised its head some 10 feet in the air and looked about. It must have been searching for prey. As the snake crossed Family Bridge, I got inside the cave with my family. We closed the door and all the windows. Our hearts beat fast as we waited.

Soon the snake was in front of the cave. We opened one window and began shooting, but all of our shots missed. Startled by the noise, the monster slipped into the reedy marsh and disappeared.

I knew then that the snake must be a boa constrictor. It was huge—about 30 feet in length! I was horrified that this monster was so close to us! I told my family that we would all have to stay inside the cave. It was not safe to go outside.

For three days, we were kept in suspense and fear. I started to wonder if the boa had left the area. But the strange way our geese and ducks were acting proved otherwise. I watched them swimming anxiously about. They cackled and flapped their wings to show how nervous they were.

Hiding in the cave was very frustrating. We had work to do outside. And our animals didn't like being locked up indoors. Still, for the sake of safety, we had to stay in. It was Grizzle, our faithful donkey, who finally saved us. Unfortunately, it was at great cost to him.

By the third day, we needed more hay for the animals. We never kept much in the cave. All of the animals' food was at the farm. I decided to send the animals to the farm under Fritz's guidance. After I tied them all together, Fritz would lead them away.

The next morning, I began tying the animals in a line. My wife opened the door before I was finished. Grizzle was eager to get out. He suddenly ran out of the cave and galloped straight for the marsh!

We called him back in vain. Fritz would have rushed after him, had I not held him back. In another moment, the snake reared up and spotted Grizzle. The dark, deadly jaws opened wide. Poor Grizzle's fate was sealed.

Swift and straight, the boa was upon him. It wound around him several times, squeezing the poor donkey tighter and tighter. All the while, the giant reptile avoided the kicks of the agonized animal.

"Shoot him, Father! Shoot him now! Save

our poor Grizzle!" the boys cried out.

"It is impossible, dear children! I'm afraid that Grizzle is lost to us forever. But I still have hopes that we can kill the snake!"

"But surely the snake is not going to swallow a whole donkey all at once, Father? That would be impossible!"

"Snakes have no teeth, only fangs," I explained. "Since they cannot chew their food, they must swallow it whole. First the boa squeezes its victim into a shapeless mass, crushing the bones. Then it begins to swallow its prey. But once it swallows Grizzle's body, the boa will be unable to move. For some time, it will use its energy for digestion. That's when we can kill him."

We watched in horror as the snake killed and ate Grizzle. It took the boa five hours to get Grizzle's body down its throat! Then the swollen snake lay stiff and still along the edge of the marsh.

The time for attack was now or never! My sons and I crept out of our cave. We shot the snake dead.

"Can we eat that snake?" Franz asked.

"Of course not!" cried his mother. "Why, don't you know that snakes are poisonous, child? It would be too dangerous."

"No, my dear wife," I said. "The boa is not poisonous. It kills its prey by crushing it. But even if it *were* poisonous, we could still eat it. We would just have to throw away the head, where the poison is stored."

The rest of that sad afternoon was spent recovering Grizzle's remains. We were determined to give our faithful donkey a proper burial. After all, he had saved our lives at the cost of his own.

The sun was going down as we skinned and stuffed the boa. We put the skin in the cave by the entrance to our library. Over the door, we wrote these words: *No donkeys admitted here.* The double meaning of this sentence pleased us all.

10 Exploring the Island

Time passed quickly. Before we knew it another year had rolled around.

"I think we should explore more of this island," I said one day. "Do you realize that we've been here three years and we still haven't seen everything?"

"Did you say three years?" the boys cried in amazement. "How is that possible?"

We decided to prepare for a trip of exploration. The whole family came along. We left early one morning and set out for the land beyond the rocks. After two hours, we stopped for a rest.

We were high on a hill overlooking a wide sandy plain. It was surrounded on all sides by a pine forest. After setting up camp, we left my wife and Franz there with Juno. The three oldest boys and the other dogs went with me.

Knips, the monkey, came with us, too—along with Ernest's eagle. As we crossed a stream, we stopped to fill our flasks with water. It was good that we did so, for we soon found that we were in a desert.

The boys were surprised at the desert landscape. We walked on for many hours, suffering in the heat. At last we reached a rock sheltered by an overhang. We were glad to rest in the shade and have lunch.

After eating, Fritz gazed out upon the plain before us. "Look!" he shouted. "Is that a party of horsemen riding toward us?"

Looking through my spyglass, I could see that the figures were actually a group of very large ostriches.

"This is lucky, indeed!" I exclaimed. "We must try to catch one of these birds. Just to have the feathers alone would be wonderful!"

As the ostriches approached, we tried to think of how we could catch one. I could see that only one of the five birds was a male. His white tail and wing feathers contrasted finely with the deep glossy black of his body. The females' bodies were brown, so the contrast of their white feathers was not so great.

I warned the boys that ostriches could be dangerous. They use their powerful legs as kicking weapons. When the ostriches came closer, we tried to keep the dogs hidden. But the dogs broke away and rushed toward the birds—who ran away with the speed of the wind! Then Ernest unhooded his eagle. The eagle singled out the male bird and killed him quickly. The sight made us very unhappy.

"Too bad we weren't able to take that glorious bird alive!" Fritz exclaimed. "It must have stood more than six feet high. Two of us could have ridden him at once!"

I told the boys all I knew about ostriches. They were very interested to hear that the ostrich makes a noise like the roar of a lion.

Just then, Jack found a slight hollow in the ground. Inside were more than 20 ostrich eggs! Each one was as large as an infant's head and weighed about three pounds. Since we could only carry two of them, we set up a landmark so we could find them again later.

Our exploration continued. Soon we arrived at a charming valley. The place was green, fruitful, and shaded by graceful trees. We rested there for a while and decided to call this valley Green Glen.

Off in the distance, we could see large herds of antelopes or buffaloes. Following the windings of the valley, we soon came to more open ground. Ernest was ahead of us with one of the dogs. We lost sight of him for a few minutes. Then we heard a cry of terror, loud barking, and deep growls!

As we rushed forward, Ernest met us. His face was as white as ashes. "It's a bear—a *bear*, Father!" he cried. "It's coming after me!"

The boy clung to me in terror. I felt his whole frame quivering.

"Courage, my son!" I said sternly. "We must prepare to defend ourselves."

Soon two enormous bears appeared. Fritz and I shot at them, but we didn't kill them. The bears were badly wounded, however. One had a broken jaw, and the other had a bullet in his shoulder.

When the dogs attacked, we stopped shooting at once since we didn't want to hit our dogs. We'd have to get closer first.

Watching for our chance, we came within a few paces of the animals. Then we fired again, and both creatures fell dead. One was shot through the head. The other was shot through the heart.

"Thank heaven!" I cried. "We've escaped the greatest danger we've come across!"

We dragged the bears' bodies into their den. Our plan was to return later to skin them. We also left the ostrich eggs behind, hidden in a sandy hole.

By sunset we got back to our camp site. We were glad to see my wife and Franz. We ate the hearty meal she had prepared for us. After telling about our day's adventures, it was time to go to sleep.

The next day we took a cart and went back to the bears' den. Skinning them was no easy job. It took several days. We smoked the meat on the spot. While we were waiting for the meat to cure, the older boys went off across the plain. My wife, Franz, and I stayed behind. We spent the time cleaning, salting, and drying the bear skins.

That evening, the older boys came back.

Their trip had been successful. They had captured two rabbits and two fawns, which they carried in bags. They had also driven an entire herd of antelopes toward the forest near Rock House. They wanted them nearby so they could hunt whenever they liked.

But best of all was the ostrich that they had managed to catch. Jack had used a lasso to bring the bird down. Then they had thrown a coat over the ostrich's head, which calmed it. Jack was looking forward to taming the enormous bird. He planned to train it the way he might train a saddle horse.

It was too late now to set out for Rock House. After tying the ostrich between two trees, we spent the rest of the evening preparing for tomorrow's departure.

11 Home Again

At dawn we headed homeward. Leading the blindfolded ostrich, we made quite a caravan. It took us two days to get back to Rock House.

On the way home, we visited our farm. The number of our pigs, goats, and poultry had increased greatly since our last visit. We decided to bring some chickens back with us.

We found that the herd of antelopes had settled in. Several times we saw the beautiful animals roaming among the trees.

At last we reached our home. We threw open windows and doors to let in the fresh air. We tied the ostrich between two bamboo posts in front of the cave.

The next morning we started trying to tame the ostrich. But all our efforts seemed in vain. A week later, he seemed as wild as ever.

I decided then to try the same plan that had tamed the eagle.

The effect of the smoke was immediate. The ostrich sank to the ground and lay still. Finally, he slowly got up and paced up and down between the bamboo posts. He was calm—but to my dismay, he refused all food! I feared he would die. For three days he pined, growing weaker and weaker each day.

"He *must* have some food!" I said to my wife. She made balls of corn flour mixed with butter and put one inside the bird's beak. He took it and looked around for more. He ate four balls. After that, his appetite returned, and he was soon strong again.

The wild nature of the bird had faded. He began to eat rice, guavas, and corn. He also took in small pebbles, which surprised Franz. I explained that all birds need to eat some kind of pebbles to digest their food.

After a month of training, our ostrich would trot, gallop, and obey the sound of our voices. He would also eat from our hands.

I made a special leather hood for the bird, with holes for its eyes and ears. I added flaps, which could easily be raised or lowered at the rider's pleasure. When both blinkers were open, the ostrich would gallop straight ahead. Close his right eye, and he turned to the left. Close his left eye, and he turned to the right. Close both, and he stood still.

I made a special saddle for the ostrich to secure the rider. I also made reins so the rider could control the bird's speed. To slow the bird down, the reins were loosened. When the reins were drawn tight, he would go fast. It was hard to remember this—as it didn't seem to make any sense. At last, however, we all learned to manage Hurricane, as we'd decided to name him.

Our field work took a lot of time. The land had been plowed and seeded. Wheat, barley, and corn were growing. On the other side of Jackal River, we had planted potatoes and many other vegetables.

I now found time for less important tasks. The boys had been asking for hats. I decided to make one and see how it turned out. I used the skin of a rat we had killed earlier. I put some India rubber over that, to make a kind of felt fabric. This I dyed a bright red. Then I stretched it on a wooden block and passed a hot iron over it. This smoothed out the nap. By next morning, I gave my wife a neat little red Swiss cap. She lined it with silk and decorated it with ribbons and ostrich feathers. Finally, we placed it on Franz's head.

Everyone was so delighted with the cap that I made some more. Soon each member of the family had one.

And so we passed month after month, year after year. Before we knew it, we were celebrating our tenth year on the island! Fritz was now a fine young man of 25, strong and active. Ernest, at 23, was mild, calm, and studious. At 20, Jack was a lot like Fritz in his personality—but more graceful and less muscular. And Franz, at 18, had some of the qualities of each of his brothers. In addition, he had great wit and a good sense of humor.

All were good, God-fearing young men. They were loving toward their mother and me and also toward one another.

# Jenny

One day Fritz came back from one of his expeditions with some very interesting news.

He had taken the boat all the way to the other side of the island. This was a spot we'd seen, but not explored. He said that he'd come to a cove, very calm and clear. Gazing into the water, he saw beds of large oysters. Thinking that they'd be good to eat, he raised up several clusters with his boat hook. Opening one up, he found a beautiful pearl inside! When he opened several more, he found a pearl in each one. He quickly gathered many more of these oysters to take home.

After stopping for lunch, Fritz continued exploring the coast. As he came to another cove, thousands of sea birds flew about him. They were screaming and flapping their wings at him. Fritz stood up and struck out with the boat hook. To his surprise, he hit one of the birds with such force that it fell to the water. Then Fritz noticed a piece of rag wrapped around one of the bird's legs. He removed it and was surprised to see English words written on it. It said, *Save the English woman from the smoking rock!*

"My dear son," I said, "let us not tell the others about this yet. It is possible that these words were written long ago. This woman might have died already. 'Smoking rock' must mean a volcano. There are none around here." But Fritz was sure that I was wrong. He was convinced that smoke could have another source besides a volcano.

The next day we all went out to Pearl Bay, the name we had chosen for the cove of large oysters. We thought we should collect the pearls in case the boys should ever return to Europe. They would need money then, and the pearls were worth a great deal.

While we were there, Fritz noticed smoke drifting from an island in the distance. He decided to take the boat out there and look around. Maybe the note had come from there!

Fritz was gone for five days. I was beginning to get worried when at last I saw the sailboat approaching. We all hurried down to the beach to wait for him. As the boat got closer and closer, we stared in amazement. We could see that he had a young woman with him!

She told us that her name was Jenny Montrose. She had been born in India, the daughter of a British officer who served there. When Jenny was three years old, her mother had died. When Jenny was 17, her father was ordered back to England. He did not wish her to travel in the ship with the troops. So he put her on a different ship that was sailing at about the same time. A week after she left Calcutta, a big storm came up.

The crew was finally forced to abandon ship and take to the boats. The boats became separated in the wild storm. Jenny's boat was capsized, and she was the only one to reach shore. A few useful things washed ashore after the wreck. Among them were some fishing supplies, knives, and other tools. There was also a chest of sailors' clothes.

She had been alone on the island for three years. She had built herself a hut. She kept a fire going constantly, hoping to attract attention. She had tamed a large bird that brought her food of all kinds, such as fish, birds, and rabbits. This bird had been her only companion. Although it often took off for long periods of time, the bird always came back. This, of course, was the bird she had sent with the message.

We welcomed Jenny into our family. My wife prepared a feast to celebrate her arrival. We used all our best china, silver, and glass. The table was set with white linen, and a vase of flowers was placed in the center. We had pineapples, oranges, apples, and pears. Deer was served, along with chicken and ham. It was, indeed, a perfect feast. Tears of joy showed the girl's appreciation.

After dinner, we went for a stroll on the beach. Jack and Franz decided to do some target practice. After setting up a barrel as a target, they fired and blew the cask into pieces. Then, as if in answer to the boys' shots, we heard three loud gunshots booming across the water from the west!

We looked at each other, speechless. Had we *really* heard guns from a strange ship?

Feelings of fear, joy, and hope rushed over us. Was it a European ship close upon our shores? Were we about to be linked once more to civilized life? Or were the strangers pirates who would rob and murder us? Were they friends who would help us? Were they enemies who would attack us? Or were they people in need of our help?

Our questions were soon answered. Within a few minutes, a ship with an English flag came into view. Fritz and I took our sailboat out to meet it. The captain welcomed us warmly. He led us to his cabin and asked us to explain why we were there.

I told him the history of the wreck and our life on the island. I talked to him about Jenny, too. It turned out that the officer knew her father. In fact, he had brought his ship to this area in hopes of finding Jenny. He said that Colonel Montrose had never given up hope of finding his daughter.

That night I had a long and serious talk

with my wife. We had to decide whether or not we really wanted to return to Europe. It didn't take us long to discover that neither one of us wanted to leave the peaceful island!

My dear wife told me that she would be happy to spend the rest of her life in New Switzerland. If I—and at least two of her sons—would stay, she would willingly part with the other two if they chose to go back to Europe. But she wanted them to send out more people to join us so we could form a prosperous colony. She also wanted to keep the name of New Switzerland, even when colonists from England came. I heartily agreed with her.

Later that day, we showed the captain and his officers our island. They were astonished at how much we had done. Some of the ship's passengers even decided to stay with us in New Switzerland!

The only thing that remained was for my sons to decide if they wanted to go or stay. Fritz decided to go to England. He wanted to bring happiness to a sad father by returning his missing daughter. Ernest chose to stay

with us in New Switzerland, and so did Jack.
The youngest boy, Franz, was eager to go to a
good school. So it was decided: Fritz, Jenny,
and Franz would soon be sailing away on the
English ship!

The captain of the ship was very pleased.
"My orders were to search for survivors of a
shipwrecked crew," he said. "Instead, I have
found survivors from *two* wrecks!"

We packed up everything that could
contribute to our children's comfort. We gave
them pearls, corals, furs, spices, and other
valuables to help them make their way in the
world. They took the private papers, money,
and jewels that had belonged to our ill-fated
captain. If possible, I told them to hand them
over to his family. And I gave information
about the wreck, with the names of the crew,
to the English captain.

Fritz was already in love. He told me that
he wanted to marry Jenny. I told him to talk
to her father about this as soon as possible.
My wife and I gladly gave them our blessing.

On the evening before they departed, I
gave Fritz the journal I had been keeping. I

told him of my fond wish that the story of our adventures might be printed and published.

"As you know, I wrote this journal for my children," I said. "But who knows? Our story might well be interesting and useful to other young people as well."

Now night has fallen. It is the last night my family will be together. Tomorrow, this final chapter of our adventures will go into the hands of my eldest son.

From afar I greet you, Europe!

And I greet you, dear old Switzerland!

Like you, may New Switzerland always be good, happy, and free!